This edition published exclusively for Alton Towers Ltd by
Macdonald & Co (Publishers) Ltd,
a member of Pergamon MCC Publishing Corporation plc,
Greater London House,
Hampstead Road,
London NW1 7QX

'Henry Hound' copyright © Alton Towers Ltd 1988
Artwork copyright © Macdonald & Co (Publishers) Ltd
Text copyright © Macdonald & Co (Publishers) Ltd

Published March 1988
Made and printed in Great Britain
ISBN 0 361 08252 5

The ADVENTURES of HENRY HOUND

Illustrated by
Mike Gordon

Written by
Greg Steddy

From an original concept by
John O'Sullivan

Trouble With Herbert

"Oh no, not again!" groaned Henry Hound, as he drew his bedroom curtains and peered out at the day.

The rain was falling cold and heavy on his window pane and a chill wind blew through the trees. Henry shivered.

"If it carries on like this I shall have to build an ark!" he muttered. "At least it would give me something to do!"

Poor Henry hated the rain. He wasn't too fond of the cold either. But what he hated most of all was being bored. He wandered downstairs and went to bring in the milk. It was then that he noticed a large brown envelope lying on the doormat.

Henry didn't get many letters so he felt rather excited. He tore open the envelope and found a letter, a yellow tee-shirt and a large key. He began to read, and as he did so his eyes opened wide in amazement.

"I don't believe it! I just don't believe it!" he repeated, and began reading bits of the letter out loud to convince himself.

"'. . . pleased to inform you . . . according to the will of your late great-uncle Hector . . . his house and lands . . . yours to occupy at your convenience . . .'"

"Mine?" said Henry to himself. "I never even met great-uncle Hector. And his house — it's huge. There must be some mistake!"

But there was no mistake. Henry had inherited Alton Towers. He sat thinking about the good news for some time, then finally leapt to his feet.

"Right, Henry," he cried, pacing excitedly up and down. "This is your lucky day. There's no time to lose!"

And with that he rushed upstairs and began to pack his things.

Soon Henry was trundling through towns and villages, past green fields and leafy lanes and leaving his old life behind him. As the afternoon shadows began to lengthen he spotted the towers and turrets of a large house through the trees.

''There it is!'' he cried excitedly. ''Home of the world-famous Henry Hound, Lord of the Manor!''

The bus stopped at the top of the drive leaving Henry to walk to the main entrance.

The house was much, much bigger than Henry had imagined. He couldn't help thinking that it was also just a teeny bit spooky. A flight of stone steps, flanked by two large stone dogs, led up to the heavy wooden doors.

''The family crest!'' chuckled Henry. ''I'd recognise that nose anywhere!''

He picked up his bags and climbed the steps to the doors. There he found a strange note:

'Greetings, Henry,' it said. 'I trust your new home is to your liking. Provision has been made for your arrival and I look forward to making your acquaintance. Yours in spirit, Herbert.'

''That's odd,'' thought Henry. ''Nobody mentioned anyone called Herbert. Oh well, I suppose I'll meet him soon enough.''

The great iron key turned easily in the lock and the door creaked open . . .

Henry's mouth dropped open in astonishment at the sight that met his eyes. In front of him was a huge room, lit by the flickering glare of a large log fire. The panelled walls were decorated with ancient weapons and shields and several suits of armour stood glinting in the corners. A large wooden staircase led to the upper rooms and a number of portraits hung along its length.

''Must be the rest of the family,'' grinned Henry, nervously. ''I didn't know there were so many of us!''

If he'd looked a little more closely, he might have had a nasty shock, for all of the portraits were watching him intently with their bright beady eyes.

However, the only thing on Henry's mind was food. He suddenly realised that he hadn't eaten a thing all day.

''But what if there's no food in the kitchen?'' he wondered, panicking slightly. ''I'll never last out until breakfast.''

11

He began to walk briskly from room to room until he found the kitchen. He paused expectantly by the larder door, then flung it open quickly. The first thing he saw was a mouse tucking into a large slice of cheddar.

"Hey!" cried Henry, indignantly. "What do you think you're doing?" The mouse froze, then started to jabber away for all he was worth.

"OK, guv, you got me this time, but times is hard, see, what with the missus and fourteen kids to feed, and there's me with this bad leg, and me dear old mum would turn in her grave if she knew I'd been caught, and . . ."

"All right, all right," interrupted Henry. "You can have the cheese. I'm not keen on it anyway."

The mouse breathed a sigh of relief.

"Bless you, squire, you're a real gent," he said. "You'll not regret it, you'll see. I'll make it up to you somehow. I'll . . ."

"Look, I've said you can have it," said Henry, impatiently. "There's no need to go on so."

The mouse calmed down and looked at Henry closely.

"Not meaning to be nosey, chief," he began. "But you're new here, aren't you? Sid's the name, by the way."

Henry introduced himself and explained about his inheritance.

"Stone me!" cried Sid. "Just wait till I tell Doris. That's the wife. She'll be dying to meet you. Then there's Kevin, that's our eldest and the twins, Ethel and . . ."

"Yes, yes, I'm sure I'll meet them all very soon," said Henry, quickly. He had just spotted some cold ham and was anxious to try it out. "You wouldn't know by any chance if Herbert is around?" he added.

"He's around all right!" laughed Sid. "That's the trouble with him! But he might see you before you see him!" And with that the mouse said goodbye and sauntered off, chuckling loudly to himself.

"I wonder what he meant by that?" thought Henry, as he cut himself a piece of ham. "Perhaps I'll find out in the morning."

As he made his way up to the master bedroom he was sure he heard someone laugh behind him. He turned quickly, but there was only a suit of armour standing in an alcove.

"I must be hearing things," he muttered, shrugging his shoulders. "It's been a pretty long day."

Henry woke feeling much refreshed. He washed and dressed and went downstairs where to his surprise he found a pot of tea and a plate of freshly buttered toast waiting for him on the table.

"Hello," called Henry, cautiously. "Is anyone about?"

But there wasn't a soul in sight. The house was as silent as the grave.

"Maybe I've got an invisible butler!" he thought, and giggled nervously. "Whoever it is, he certainly knows how to make good toast!" grinned Henry, tucking in. He certainly wasn't going to let it spoil his breakfast.

Feeling much better, but none the wiser, Henry decided to take a stroll around the grounds. He hadn't gone very far when there was a crashing sound in the trees overhead. He looked up and was promptly flattened by a grey furry creature that landed on him from a great height.

"Gosh, dreadfully sorry, old chap. Must be losing my touch!"

Henry opened his eyes and found himself face to face with a rather dazed squirrel.

"Didn't hurt you, did I?" asked the squirrel.

"Oh, I daresay I'll survive," muttered Henry, dusting himself down painfully. "I'll just be a bit more careful next time I walk under the trees!"

"Haven't spotted you around these parts before," said the squirrel, gathering up his fallen acorns. "Here on holiday, are you?"

"As a matter of fact I've just moved into the big house," said Henry, trying not to sound annoyed.

"Well, give my regards to Herbert when you see him," said the squirrel with a grin, and dashed back up the tree.

"I must be the only person around here who *hasn't* seen him," cried Henry, crossly.

"Oh, you will," chuckled the squirrel. "You will!" And he crashed off into the branches.

"This is absurd!" snorted Henry. "I'm going to search that house from top to bottom until I find out what's going on around here. I'm sure this Herbert has got a lot to do with it!"

Back in the house once more, Henry decided to explore every nook and cranny for a clue to the mystery. He hunted high and low, searching through rooms and hallways and discovering new passages and staircases until he became quite lost. Every so often he would stop suddenly and listen. Was that a door slamming? Could he hear footsteps up ahead? Once he was sure he heard someone laughing, but he found nothing.

"This is hopeless," sighed Henry at last. "There can't be anyone else living here."

He leant against a wall to get his breath back. Behind him, a secret door swivelled inwards and he fell with a startled cry into a dark passage beyond.

"Wh-Where am I?" he wailed, his heart pounding. "I can't see a thing!"

He groped his way down the passage and came to an old door. All at once, he stopped dead in his tracks and the hair on the back of his neck stood on end. He could distinctly hear a deep, gloomy moaning and the sound was coming from the other side of the door!

Summoning up all his courage, he pushed the door quietly open and crept into the room. An extraordinary sight met his eyes. The room was lit by candlelight and at the far end was a strange figure playing a tuba. Henry knew at once that there was something funny about the figure, but he couldn't quite work out what it was.

"Come in, dear boy," boomed the figure, looking up and smiling. "Wonderful to meet you after all this time. It's been so deadly dull around here just lately."

He got up and Henry almost fainted with fright. He could see right through him!

"H-H-H-Herbert?" quavered Henry, trembling all over. "B-B-But y-you're a g-g-ghost!"

"Well of course I am," chuckled Herbert. "Didn't anyone tell you? The whole house is haunted — but I'll introduce you to the others later."

Henry felt a bit better.

"Don't worry, you'll soon get used to us," chuckled Herbert. "Besides, it can be quite handy knowing someone who can walk through things!"

"I hadn't thought of that," said Henry, and laughed out loud.

"That's better!" cried Herbert. "We'll have great fun here! I haven't had a friend for centuries — except for the other ghosts, of course. But, you know, after a while *they* just bore you to death!"

"I bet they do!" giggled Henry. Perhaps living with ghosts might be fun after all, he thought to himself. His eyes shone at the thought of the adventures that lay ahead of him in his new home with all his new friends.

"I can hardly wait!" he said happily.

Things that go BUMP in the night!

''Good morning, Henry,'' said a familiar voice. ''Another fine day!''

Henry looked up from his breakfast and smiled as Herbert appeared through the kitchen wall.

Since the shock of his first encounter with his ghostly companion, Henry had become used to Herbert popping up unexpectedly. In fact, it was really rather comforting to know that Herbert was never very far away.

"How are you liking your new home?" asked the ghost. "I daresay this old house takes a bit of getting used to!"

"Well, life is certainly never dull with you around!" grinned Henry.

"I've always been a little high-spirited!" chuckled Herbert. "Which reminds me — it's about time I introduced you to the other ghosts here. They're dying to meet you! I've arranged a little party for this evening. You can meet everyone then."

Henry was very excited at the prospect. He hadn't really got used to having one ghost around, let alone a whole house full!

As the evening approached, Henry got ready for the party and made his way to the banqueting hall.

"Ah Henry, come and join us," cried Herbert, as Henry walked in. "We're nearly all here."

Henry had never seen such a strange assortment of characters sitting round a table. They all stopped talking and eyed him curiously.

"Allow me to present our resident knight, Percy," said Herbert, indicating an upright figure in full armour.

Next to him sat a transparent gentleman in Elizabethan costume, with his head tucked under his arm.

"Sir Walter, at your service," said the gentleman, and bowed slightly. "I live in the west wing — like Algernon here."

The skeleton next to him grinned broadly. At that moment there was a deafening crash, and a tall, pale figure in a black cloak came hurtling through the window.

"This is the Count," said Herbert. "He's a bit batty, but I'm sure you'll like him!"

"Sorry I'm late," apologised the Count. "I had to go to the dentist!"

With all the introductions over, the food and drink was brought in, and everyone began to dig in — everyone that is except for Algernon.

"Nothing for me thanks," he chuckled. "I'm on a diet!"

Everyone started to laugh. No-one noticed the small, dark object emerging slowly from the surface of the lake outside. It was the periscope of a mini-submarine!

Inside the submarine was none other than the notorious criminal, Billy the Weasel, and his dim-witted henchmen, Knuckles and Scarface.

"Excellent, excellent," said Billy, peering through the periscope. "This is the place all right."

"Where are we, boss?" whined Knuckles, miserably. "It's cold and dark and . . ."

"Listen, birdbrain," snarled Billy, peering through the periscope. "Just remember that if it wasn't for me, you'd still be in jail, right?"

"Right, boss," mumbled Knuckles, apologetically. "So what's the plan?"

"Yeah, what's in it for us, chief?" added Scarface.

"OK, you two," said Billy, slowly. "Pay attention! This is Alton Towers and they say there's priceless treasure hidden somewhere. No-one knows exactly where it is, but it's supposed to be worth a fortune!"

"What if we can't find it?" asked Knuckles. "Shouldn't we have a map or something?"

"We'll just keep looking until we do find it," said Billy. "It looks like no-one's lived here for years, so we won't be disturbed."

"Are you quite sure, boss?" asked Knuckles, nervously looking through the periscope. "It looks really creepy to me!"

"Scared of the dark, are we?" sneered Billy. "You'll be telling me you believe in ghosts next! Now come on, let's get moving."

They climbed out of the submarine and Billy set off towards the house, his two henchmen following some way behind.

"This place gives me the creeps," muttered Scarface, under his breath. "I'm sure I saw a light flickering in one of those windows just now."

"Keep quiet, numbskull!" hissed Billy. "And hurry up — we've got to make our getaway before dawn!"

The crooks tested several of the downstairs windows until they found one with a loose catch. Knuckles forced it open with a crowbar and they all crawled inside. Billy gave a low whistle as he shone his flashlight around the room.

"Look at all this lot!" he whispered excitedly. "There's enough stuff here to make us all rich ten times over — even if we don't find the hidden treasure."

"Couldn't we just grab some of the silver and run for it?" whimpered Knuckles. "I keep getting the horrible feeling that we're being watched."

"Don't be daft!" snarled Billy. "There's no-one here except us. Now let's split up and get to work!"

Knuckles and Scarface tiptoed uneasily away in opposite directions — both wishing they'd never agreed to come. After a few minutes, Scarface found himself in the kitchen, and the thought of food crossed his mind. He pulled open the larder door and Sid the mouse, frozen for a second in the torch beam, scuttled away across the floor.

"Waagh!!" shrieked Scarface. "A mouse!" And he rushed blindly back the way he had come as fast as his legs would carry him!

He hurtled around a corner and ran full tilt into a suit of armour standing at the top of a flight of stairs. With a loud cry, he tumbled head over heels to the bottom, the armour flying down and landing on him with a deafening crash.

''What was that noise?'' asked Henry suddenly, his keen ears picking up the distant clatter. ''Sounded like something falling over.''

''Maybe we've got ghosts!'' chuckled Herbert, and the whole company roared with laughter.

At that moment Sid appeared through a hole in the skirting board.

''We've got burglars in the house,'' he panted breathlessly. ''You'd better do something before they pinch everything.''

''Don't you worry,'' said Herbert, with a mischievous glint in his eye. ''We can have some fun here. Come on, Algernon! You too, Percy!''

Knuckles, meanwhile, had heard all the noise and was desperately looking for the way out. He had had quite enough for one night.

"M-Maybe th-that's it," he stammered, spotting a door at the end of a passage. He pulled it open quickly and Algernon the skeleton came leaping out, wailing and rattling his bones.

Knuckles went white as a sheet, turned and ran for his life, yelling in terror.

At the bottom of the stairs, Scarface groaned painfully as he slowly sat up.

"Here, let me help you," boomed a deep voice behind him. He froze as he felt a cold, heavy hand on his shoulder and whirled round to see the suit of armour bending over him.

"Y-You can't be real!" he cried, scrambling dizzily to his feet. "Y-You're just a s-suit of armour!"

Percy shook his head slowly and gave a loud chuckle. Scarface wasn't prepared to stay and argue, and rushed off with a wild yell.

Billy could hear all the commotion and shook his head wearily.

''I knew I shouldn't have brought those idiots along,'' he muttered, stuffing some candlesticks into his sack. ''Still, it means I can have all the loot for myself!''

He stopped dead as Herbert suddenly burst through the wall in front of him.

''The property of Henry Hound I believe!'' he cried sternly, glaring at the sack of stolen goods. ''Give it back at once!''

''Not likely, mate!'' said Billy through clenched teeth, trying hard not to show how frightened he was. ''You'll have to come and get it!''

Herbert flew at Billy and passed right through him. The villain gave a startled cry and made a bolt for the door. Before Herbert could stop him he was gone.

Billy stumbled out into the night, clutching the sack, and found the others down by the lake, still wailing and gibbering in fright. He looked out over the water and his eyes narrowed in disbelief. The submarine had gone!

"I-I think it's sunk, boss," stammered Knuckles, miserably. "Wh-What are we going to do?"

"You blundering fools!" cried Billy, in a furious temper. "One of you must have left the hatch door open!"

The two crooks looked at the ground sheepishly.

"We'll just have to spend the night in the woods until it gets light," snapped Billy. "We'll never find our way out of here in the dark."

"Don't worry, Henry," said Herbert. "They won't get far, you'll see!"

"I'd better go and look for them all the same," said Henry. "They shouldn't be too difficult to follow."

He set out as soon as dawn began to break and trotted off into the woods.

"Morning, Henry," cried a rabbit, popping its head out of a hole in the ground. "You're up early. What's the rush?"

Henry quickly explained about the robbery and the three villains still at large.

"I'll tell the others," offered the rabbit. "We'll soon flush them out!"

"Thanks," said Henry. "I'll see if I can pick up their trail."

The three crooks had spent a cold, uncomfortable night huddled under an old oak tree. Billy shook the others roughly awake.

"Come on, you two," he hissed urgently. "We've got to get out of here before it's too . . ."

He stopped short as a fir cone struck him right on the nose. Another hit him on the ear. Suddenly they were being pelted from all sides.

Word had quickly spread through the woods, and the squirrels had lost no time in finding the villains.

"They're onto us, chief!" cried Scarface, in alarm. "Let's run for it!"

They raced blindly through the trees and had just reached the edge of the woods when they saw Henry.

"We've been spotted, boss!" cried Knuckles. "We'll never make it!"

"Quiet, you idiot," snapped Billy. "It's only a dog. We'll escape in the cable cars. He'll never follow us up there!"

The villains rushed into the Skyride station and leapt into the nearest cable car. Within seconds they were gliding away over the park.

"Oh no," groaned Henry, in dismay. "They're getting away. I'll never catch them now!"

He burst into the station, intent on following the thieves, but in his haste he tripped over his own feet and crashed into the mechanism, hitting his head on a large red button. Immediately all the cable cars ground to a halt, trapping the crooks way up in the air.

"Well done, my boy!" beamed Herbert later on that same day.

"So the police arrived and took those scoundrels off to jail, eh? Best place for them, I say!"

"And we managed to get all the stolen silver back," added Henry.

"Thanks to you," said Herbert.

"Oh it wasn't all down to me," grinned Henry, modestly. "Once those villains tried to interrupt our party, they didn't stand a ghost of a chance!"

Henry and the Hidden Treasure

As dawn was breaking bright and early one morning over Alton Towers, Henry Hound tossed and turned restlessly in his sleep. He had a nasty feeling that something was wrong, but he wasn't quite sure what it was. He slowly became aware of a strange rumbling sound, quite faint at first, but gradually becoming louder and louder. He tried to concentrate, but felt oddly weak and feeble. Suddenly he realised what was wrong: the rumbling noise was coming from his own stomach — he was HUNGRY!

"I knew I should have had supper before I went to bed!" he thought, quickly pulling on his clothes. "Right now I could eat a horse. Maybe two!"

Henry ran downstairs to the kitchen and flung open the larder door. A terrible sight met his eyes. The larder was empty! "Oh no!" he cried, staring in disbelief. "I forgot to go shopping yesterday!"

He raced frantically around the kitchen, looking in every cupboard and drawer he could see. In each one he found the same — nothing! He came to the last one, a dusty old drawer in the corner, and wrenched it open. Inside was Sid, wrestling manfully with an ancient and very smelly piece of Stilton cheese.

"Blimey, guv!" cried Sid, guiltily. "Gave me a rare old fright, you did! And how long have you had this bit of cheese? It's as tough as old boots!"

"Looks like you've found the only scrap of food in the house," said Henry, miserably.

"Don't I know it!" said the mouse. "The wife'll go mad when I come back with nothing for breakfast! I've hunted high and low, and all I could find was this old cheese. Oh, and this, of course — but I can't eat it, I've tried!"

He handed Henry an old roll of parchment. It was covered in dust, and slightly chewed in one corner.

"What is it?" asked Henry, curiously opening it out.

"Don't ask me, guv," said Sid. "Found it at the back of this drawer here. Been there for donkey's years, if you ask me!"

"It looks like a map of the house and grounds," said Henry, peering at it closely. "It must be really old — Herbert probably knows what it means."

"Very interesting, I'm sure," said Sid. "But it doesn't show me where I'm going to get the wife's breakfast. And unless I'm back pretty sharpish, I'm really going to be in the doghouse — if you'll pardon the expression."

Henry watched Sid scurry off, then had another look at the map. There was some writing on it in a strange, flowery script, but it was too faint for him to read.

Henry decided to ask Herbert about the map. He soon found him in the library.

"Greetings, my dear boy," cried the ghost, cheerfully. "What's that you've got there?"

Henry showed him the map. Herbert stared at it for a few seconds, then his eyes opened wide in amazement.

"This is quite remarkable," he said. "Have you got any idea what this is, Henry? Where on earth did you find it?"

Henry told him the story and the ghost chuckled merrily.

"Well, bless my soul!" he exclaimed. "So it's been here all the time!"

"But what exactly is it?" asked Henry.

"This, my dear chap," explained the ghost, "is none other than the long-lost treasure map of another of your famous ancestors — the notorious pirate, Captain Horatio Hound!"

"A treasure map!" echoed Henry. "How exciting! But what sort of treasure is it?"

"No-one really knows," said Herbert. "But it's rumoured to be something that Horatio valued above all else. The trouble was that he was very forgetful. He drew the map so that he could remember where he'd hidden the treasure — but then he forgot where he'd hidden the map!"

"So the treasure's never been found," cried Henry, excitedly. "And we've got the map!"

Henry looked again at the yellowed parchment and suddenly frowned.

"But this map's no good," he sighed in disappointment. "The treasure isn't marked on it. There's only this writing — and I can't read it."

Herbert studied it carefully for a moment and then chuckled. "I think it's some sort of game," he said. "I've heard that Horatio was a bit of a joker. Listen to this:

"'Roses are red, violets are blue,
If you can't find my picture, you won't have a clue.'"

"What does it mean?" asked Henry, blankly. "I don't understand."

"Don't you see?" said Herbert. "It's a clue to where the treasure lies. All we have to do to start with is find Horatio's picture."

"That shouldn't be too difficult," said Henry. "He must be among the portraits above the stairs. Let's go and have a look."

Sure enough, they soon found a picture of Horatio, splendidly dressed in his pirate clothes. Henry took it down and examined it closely.

"There's nothing here," he said sadly. "Someone must have beaten us to it."

"Try the wall behind the picture," suggested Herbert.

Henry ran his paws over the smooth stonework and gave a

cry of surprise.

"Hey! One of these stones moves!" he said, sliding it back to reveal a small hole. He reached in and pulled out a metal box.

"I've found it," he cried in delight. "I've found the treasure!"

He fumbled with the catch and pulled open the lid. Inside was nothing but a rusty old key and a small slip of paper.

"That's not treasure," he sighed. "Just another clue, by the look of it." He picked up the paper and read out the message written on it:

"'Here's a key, and here's a rhyme.
  The next clue you must find in time.'

"I don't get it," muttered Henry. "In time for what, I wonder?"

At that moment there was a light tapping sound and Sir Walter popped his head around the door.

"Good morning, gentlemen," he said gravely. "Have either of you got an aspirin?"

"Whatever's the matter?" asked Henry. "You look terrible!"

"I've got a dreadful headache," groaned Sir Walter. "I went to a Halloween party last night with Percy and the Count. I knew I should have kept off the spirits!"

As he spoke the great bell in the clock tower began to chime the hour.

"Oh no!" cried Sir Walter, wincing at the sound. "Twelve o'clock. That's all I need!" He stumbled off, clutching his hands over his ears.

"Poor Sir Walter," chuckled Henry. "I think he's overdone it this time." He paused, and suddenly jumped. "Of course! Time! Clock! That's what the rhyme means. The next clue's hidden in a clock!"

"There's an old grandfather clock in the drawing room," said Herbert. "It's been in the house for years. Perhaps it's in there!"

They raced off to the drawing room and Henry began to search expectantly inside the clock. But there was no sign of another clue. He was just about to give up when Sid scuttled down the pendulum.

"Still looking, eh?" he said cheerfully. "Not a scrap of food in here though. Just this bit of old paper!"

Henry grabbed it eagerly.

"That's just what I'm looking for!" he cried, opening it quickly. It was yet another riddle:

'First the map, and then the key.
Now look for a sign at the hollow tree.'

Henry's heart sank.

"There must be thousands of hollow trees out there in the woods," he said. "How am I supposed to find the right one?"

"If it's been there since Horatio was around, then it must be pretty old by now," suggested Herbert. "There are some big old oaks down by the river — if I were you, I'd start looking there!"

43

Henry set out, clutching the map and key, and feeling just a little bit grumpy: partly because he was getting tired of Horatio's silly clues, partly because he still hadn't eaten anything and was now feeling ravenous!

He hadn't gone far into the woods when he came upon a fat squirrel tucking into a pile of acorns.

"Morning, Henry!" he called. "Nothing like a good brisk walk after lunch, eh?"

Henry nodded politely and wondered vaguely what acorns tasted like.

"Actually," he said, "I'm looking for a hollow tree. Do you know if there are any around here?"

"Lots of them are hollow," grinned the squirrel. "That's where most of us live. But I wouldn't have thought you'd be looking for a new house already!"

"Very funny," said Henry, crossly. "Whoever heard of a dog living in a tree?"

"I knew one once," said the squirrel. "But he must have been lost. He was barking up the wrong tree!" And he rolled on the floor, howling with laughter.

"I'm looking for a special tree," said Henry, impatiently. "Very old — even older than your jokes."

"There's an old oak not far from here," said the squirrel. "Maybe that's the one you want. Come on, I'll show you!"

He led Henry down to the river and pointed out an ancient tree on the other side. Its branches were old and twisted, and there was a dark, gaping hole in the side of its trunk.

"I suppose I'll have to wade across it," grumbled Henry. He wasn't very fond of water — especially if it was cold! He had nearly reached the other side, when he slipped on the mud and fell backwards with an almighty splash.

"Oh no!" he cried. "The map — it's soaking wet!"

Henry clambered out of the water and unrolled the parchment carefully. To his amazement, a red cross slowly began to appear — and he was standing at the spot! He walked over to the hollow tree and peered cautiously into the hole. It was overgrown with twigs and leaves and was very dark.

"This is no good," muttered Henry. "I can't see a . . . waagh!"

He gave a loud cry as he leant over too far and toppled headlong into the hole. He crashed down and landed with a painful bump on the soil below.

"Where on earth am I?" he muttered, brushing twigs and dirt from his fur. He stepped forward and stubbed his toe on something hard and heavy. As his eyes grew accustomed to the gloom, he suddenly realised what it was.

"A treasure chest!" he cried, scarcely daring to believe his luck. He fumbled hastily for the key and it grated stiffly in the lock. He took a deep breath and slowly raised the lid . . .

Back at the house, the ghosts were terribly excited when Henry told them the news.

"Well, come along," said Herbert, breathlessly. "Tell us what you found!"

"You're never going to believe it!" laughed Henry. "Something I'd never have expected!"

"Gold and silver?" guessed Herbert.

"No."

"Diamonds and rubies?" suggested Sir Walter.

"No."

"What was it then?" said Herbert, impatiently.

"Well," grinned Henry. "After all these years, Captain Horatio Hound's long-lost treasure turns out to be . . . his famous BONE collection!"

There was a stunned silence for a second or two, then everyone began to laugh.

"And since I still haven't eaten today," chuckled Henry, "I reckon old Horatio's treasure is absolutely priceless!"

HIGH FLYING HOUND

"You sound happy this morning, chief," said Sid, nibbling on a piece of left-over bacon rind.

Henry stopped whistling for a second.

"And why shouldn't I be?" he replied cheerfully. "It's a wonderful morning, I've just had a splendid breakfast, and now I intend to sit in the sun and do a spot of fishing until lunchtime!"

"I thought that maybe you were excited about the circus coming to town," said Sid. "Everyone's talking about it."

"It arrives this morning, doesn't it?" asked Henry.

"That's right, guv," said the mouse. "Thought I might take the wife and kids along this evening. There's nothing on the telly!"

"Well, mind you don't scare the elephants," chuckled Henry. "See you later."

He sorted out his fishing rod and bait, packed some chocolate, a couple of apples, a packet of biscuits, some sandwiches, a cake and a bottle of lemonade — just in case he felt a bit peckish later on — and set off.

He soon found himself a comfortable spot under a willow tree, set up his line and sat down.

"This is the life," he murmured, and sighed contentedly. He leaned back against the tree and closed his eyes, dreaming of large fat trout. After a while it seemed that he could hear faint cries for help and he stirred lazily.

"That's funny," he thought. "Trout can't speak!"

"Help! Help! Save me!" cried a voice, much louder and nearer. "I can't swim!"

Henry shook his head and looked around him. This was no dream — it was really happening!

49

Right
in front of him,
splashing and choking
as she was swept along in
the water, was another dog!
And further upstream Henry could
just see two figures sitting astride a
log and paddling furiously towards the dog
in the water.

"Help!" she cried. "Don't let them catch me!"

Henry leapt to his feet and grabbed his fishing rod. "Here, hold on to this!" he called anxiously. "I'll pull you in!"

The stranger grabbed Henry's fishing rod and was hauled, gasping and spluttering, onto the bank.

"We can't stop here!" she panted. "They'll catch us!"

So saying, she charged off into the woods with Henry close behind. After a few minutes she stopped and listened. "I think we've lost them!" she sighed.

"You've certainly lost me!" said Henry. "What on earth is going on?"

"It's a long story!" said the stranger. "But the truth is — I've run away!"

"Who from?" asked Henry, his curiosity aroused.

"The circus," replied the dog, shivering with cold. "It seemed so exciting at first, performing in front of all those people. But then the circus was bought by new owners and they treated us very badly. I was so unhappy I decided to escape."

"What sort of act did you do?" asked Henry.

"I was part of an acrobatic team: Henrietta the High-Flying Hound!" she said.

"Henrietta?" said Henry, in surprise. "What a coincidence — my name's Henry! Pleased to meet you," he added, smiling shyly.

"Thank you, Henry, for saving my life!" said Henrietta, and gave him a kiss on the cheek.

Henry blushed.

"It was nothing really," he said modestly. "Besides, it's not often that I get chance to help a damsel in distress!"

"It's lucky for me that you were there," said Henrietta, with a shy smile. "I don't know what I'd have done without you!"

"But how did you come to be in the water?" asked Henry.

"The circus people were after me," explained Henrietta. "I ran into the park to give them the slip, but I was going so fast I slipped and fell into the water."

"I hope they're not still following you," said Henry, anxiously. "You'd better come home with me and lie low until they've gone."

They set off quickly, with Henry leading the way.

"I'm sure we've lost them," he said confidently. "You don't have to worry about a . . ."

His words were cut short as a large net suddenly swished through the air, trapping them both completely.

"Hey! What's going on?" cried Henry, in alarm. "I can't move!"

He spun round and saw a huge, bald-headed man dressed in a leopard skin bending over and peering at them closely.

"I've caught her, boss," he cried triumphantly. "In fact, I've got two of them!"

"Nice work, Hercules," said a voice nearby. "And make sure they don't escape!"

A tall, thin man with a moustache leered at them nastily.

"Just you let us go this minute!" shouted Henry, struggling to break free. "Or I'll get very cross!"

"Save your breath, my friend," sneered the man. "You'll make a fine addition to my circus, you and your new little friend here. But first I must think of a suitable punishment — she obviously needs to be taught a lesson!"

Henrietta whimpered as Hercules picked them up in the net and slung them over one shoulder.

"Don't worry," said Henry. "They won't get away with this. I'll think of something — I hope!"

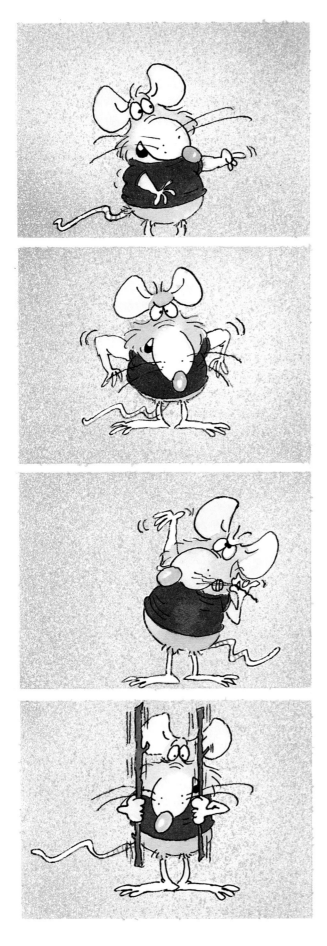

Back at the house, the ghosts were clustered anxiously around Sid. "So tell us what happened to Henry," said Algernon.

"Well, I heard it from one of the squirrels," panted the mouse excitedly.

"There was this geezer, see, great big horrible bloke, he was dressed in a leopard skin. And he catches Henry in this net, him and this other dog that rescued from the river."

"Then this tall smarmy bloke says to take them back to the circus and put them in the show."

"He locked them in a cage behind the circus tent. Mentioned teaching them a lesson."

"This is serious," said Percy. "Henry's in trouble and needs our help. We'll have to think of a way to rescue him — and his new friend."

"But what can we do?" said Sir Walter. "We can't just walk in and ask for Henry back. They might capture us too!"

"If I may make a suggestion?" said a deep voice behind them.

They all turned round to see the Count standing by the window.

"Hello, Count," said Percy. "I didn't hear you come in."

"Exactly!" said the Count, with a smile. "And that is all part of my plan. I could slip into the circus unnoticed in my, er, evening wear. Pay them a flying visit, so to speak!"

"But how will you get Henry out?" asked Sir Walter. "There's bound to be someone on guard."

"Oh, I daresay I could frighten them off," grinned the Count. "I can be a real pain in the neck sometimes!"

Meanwhile, Henry and Henrietta had been locked in a cage behind the circus tent. They sat looking miserably through the bars, wondering how they might escape, but their chances looked slim. Sitting opposite their cage was Hercules the strong man.

"What are we going to do, Henry?" asked Henrietta, hopefully. "You're the one with all the good ideas."

"I wish I knew," groaned Henry. "I can never think straight on an empty stomach. When are they going to feed us?"

"I told you they were cruel," said Henrietta. "It's their way of punishing us for escaping."

"But I didn't escape in the first place," protested Henry. "All I did was get caught!"

"Keep quiet, you two," said Hercules, lumbering to his feet. "The boss said I was to make sure you don't get up to any tricks while he's away."

"Couldn't we have something to eat?" asked Henry. "We've not had any food all day!"

"Not unless the boss says so," said Hercules. "He'd only shout at me if he found out."

"I promise I won't tell him," said Henry, hopefully.

At that moment, a mysterious dark figure appeared silently behind the cage. Henrietta was the first to notice it, and whimpered with fright.

"Ssh!" said Henry, giving her paw a reassuring squeeze. "It's a friend of mine. He'll soon have us out of here!"

"Hey! What's going on?" muttered Hercules, suspiciously. "Come out, whoever you are."

He moved closer, but then cried out in fright as a large black bat swooped down from nowhere and flew at his face. He turned to run, but tripped and fell heavily, the bunch of keys flying in all directions.

"Waagh! Mummy! Help!" bawled Hercules, flailing wildly at the bat as it swooped to attack him again.

He rushed off screaming and yelling, with the bat in hot pursuit. Seconds later, the Count unlocked the door of the cage.

"Quickly now," he whispered urgently. "Back to the house, before the circus owner gets back. I'll give this big baby a run for his money while you make your getaway."

"Thanks, Count," said Henry. "You were terrific! See you back at the house. Come on, Henrietta, there's no time to lose!"

They barely had time to slip away, before the circus owner returned and strode expectantly over to the cage.

"Now, my fine friends," he leered. "Time to start rehearsing for your act tonight."

He stopped short when he saw that the cage was empty, and gave a cry of rage.

"Hercules, you moron!" he bellowed. "Where the devil are you? You've let those wretched dogs escape!"

He stomped off, shouting and cursing, until he found Hercules still gibbering with fright.

"A v-vampire, b-boss," he stammered. "It attacked me!"

"Don't be ridiculous, you incompetent buffoon!" snarled the circus owner, furiously. "There's no such thing. You'll have to think of a better excuse than that. And don't just stand there blubbering — let's get after them. I can make a fortune with those dogs!"

Henry and Henrietta had just reached the front door of the house, when Henry looked over his shoulder and to his dismay saw a fast car speeding up the drive.

"Oh no!" he cried. "We've been followed. It's those circus people again!"

"Quick, you two, come in and hide upstairs," said Herbert, suddenly appearing at the door. "We've got a little reception committee planned for those jokers!"

Hercules rang the bell nervously and the door creaked open.

"You rang?" inquired the Count solemnly, and ushered them inside. "Th-That's him, boss!" cried Hercules. "Th-The vampire!"

The circus owner smacked him sharply round the head.

"Do excuse this twit," he said acidly. "He gets very excitable. Now I'll come straight to the point. Two of my dogs have escaped from the circus and I have reason to believe that they're hiding here."

"Oh, do you now?" boomed Herbert, suddenly appearing through the wall. "We'll see about that!"

"Waagh!" screamed Hercules. "A g-ghost! Let me out of here!"

He turned to run, but Percy stood blocking the entrance, and waving his axe menacingly. He made a break for the nearest door, but recoiled in terror as Algernon burst through it, wailing and moaning.

"I suggest you may have made a mistake," said Sir Walter, drifting towards them with his head under his arm.

"Er-er, m-maybe you're r-right," quavered the circus owner, backing away hastily. "C-come on, Hercules. They can keep the d-dogs!"

They made a bolt for the door and raced off down the drive without looking back.

"So good of you to call," grinned the Count, and flashed his teeth wickedly.

The other ghosts all roared with laughter.

"OK, Henry, you can come out now," chuckled Herbert. "We've certainly seen the last of those two rogues!"

Henry led Henrietta into the room and introduced her to the others.

"Thank you all so much," she said shyly. "I was a bit scared at first, but I knew I'd be all right with Henry around."

"Do you hear that, dear boy?" beamed Herbert. "In that case, I think Henrietta should stay here from now on. What do you say?"

"I'd like that very much," said Henry, blushing to the tips of his ears.

"So would I," said Henrietta, and smiled.

"That's settled then," cried Herbert. "Here's to Henry and Henrietta — Lord and Lady of Alton Towers!"

"Here's to us all," laughed Henry. "Now let's have dinner. I'm starving!"